The Yellow Balloon

13

'9

First published 2005
Evans Brothers Limited
2A Portman Mansions
Chiltern St
London W1U 6NR

British Library Cataloguing in Publication Data

Orme, Helen
    The yellow balloon. – (Zig zag)
    1. Children's stories – Pictorial works
    I. Title
    823.9'14 [J]

ISBN 0237529483
13-digit ISBN (from 1 January 2007) 9780237529482

Printed in China by WKT Company Ltd

Series Editor: Nick Turpin
Design: Robert Walster
Production: Jenny Mulvanny
Series Consultant: Gill Matthews

The Yellow Balloon

by Helen Bird

illustrated by Simona Dimitri

Evans

There was a balloon race
at Michael's school.

The balloons had
a postcard tied to
them – like this:

IF FOUND, PLEASE SEND TO
MICHAEL THOMAS
34 ELM DRIVE
NEWTOWN
AR45 8GF

"I bet mine will go the furthest!"
said Michael.

"One, two, three, go!"
The wind blew the balloons
high into the air.

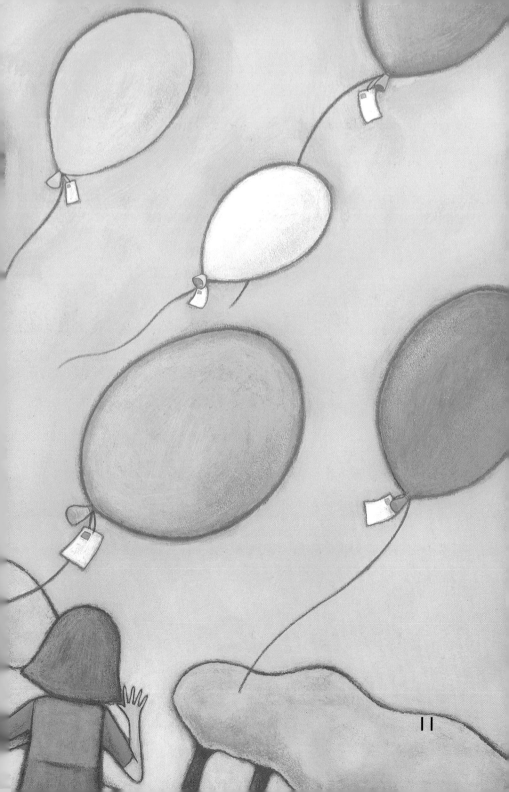

11

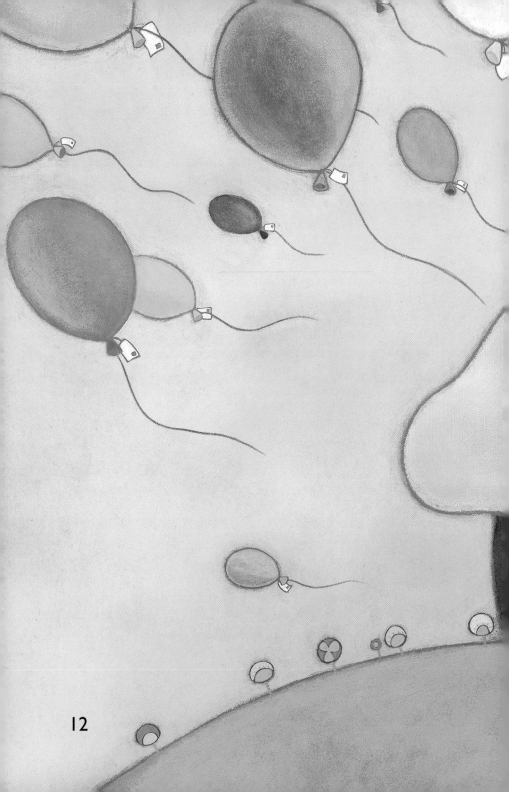

Michael's balloon didn't go
very high.

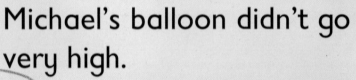

13

It came down and down...

...and got tangled up on a truck!

17

The truck drove out
of the town...

19

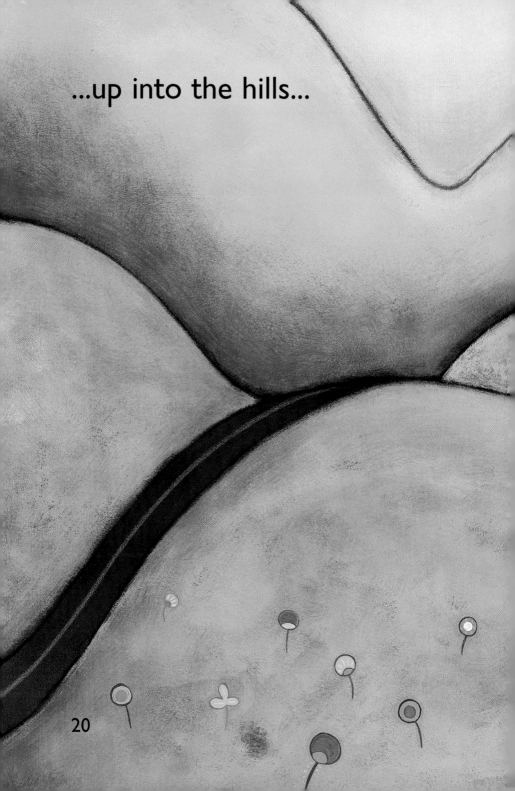

...up into the hills...

20

21

...on and on
through the
night.

The truck crossed the sea.

The truck driver found
the balloon.
"I'll post this," he thought.

Michael didn't think his
balloon had gone very far.

But it had gone further than anyone else's!

If found, please send to
Michael Thomas
34 Elm Drive
NEWTOWN
AR45 8GF

Why not try reading another ZigZag book?

Dinosaur Planet　　　　　　　ISBN: 0 237 52667 0
by David Orme and Fabiano Fiorin

Tall Tilly　　　　　　　　　　ISBN: 0 237 52668 9
by Jillian Powell and Tim Archbold

Batty Betty's Spells　　　　　ISBN: 0 237 52669 7
by Hilary Robinson and Belinda Worsley

The Thirsty Moose　　　　　　ISBN: 0 237 52666 2
by David Orme and Mike Gordon

The Clumsy Cow　　　　　　　ISBN: 0 237 52656 5
by Julia Moffatt and Lisa Williams

Open Wide!　　　　　　　　　ISBN: 0 237 52657 3
by Julia Moffatt and Anni Axworthy

Too Small　　　　　　　　　　ISBN 0 237 52777 4
by Kay Woodward and Deborah van de Leijgraaf

I Wish I Was An Alien　　　　ISBN 0 237 52776 6
by Vivian French and Lisa Williams

The Disappearing Cheese　　ISBN 0 237 52775 8
by Paul Harrison and Ruth Rivers

Terry the Flying Turtle　　　ISBN 0 237 52774 X
by Anna Wilson and Mike Gordon

Pet To School Day　　　　　　ISBN 0 237 52773 1
by Hilary Robinson and Tim Archbold

The Cat in the Coat　　　　　ISBN 0 237 52772 3
by Vivian French and Alison Bartlett

Pig in Love　　　　　　　　　ISBN 0 237 52950 5
by Vivian French and Tim Archbold

The Donkey That Was Too Fast　ISBN 0 237 52949 1
by David Orme and Ruth Rivers

The Yellow Balloon　　　　　ISBN 0 237 52948 3
by Helen Bird and Simona Dimitri

Hamish Finds Himself　　　　ISBN 0 237 52947 5
by Jillian Powell and Belinda Worsley

Flying South　　　　　　　　ISBN 0 237 52946 7
by Alan Durant and Kath Lucas

Croc by the Rock　　　　　　ISBN 0 237 52945 9
by Hilary Robinson and Mike Gordon

32